Her Perfect Scoundrel

A ROGUE'S KISS

AMANDA MARIEL

This is a work of fiction. Names, characters, organizations, places, events, and incidents are either products of the author's imagination or are used fictitiously.

Her Perfect Scoundrel was previously published as Rogue of Her Heart in the Christmas Anthology How The Rogue Stole Christmas and has been re-edited for its solo release.

Published by Brook Ridge Press

Prologue

Yorkshire, *England*
May, 1819

Drat, drat, drat! Lady Celia Kendal did not appear a lady at all as she held her skirts and kicked the carriage wheel. Her brother Charles, the Duke of Selkirk, would be furious when he discovered what she'd done.

Her companion, Rosie, poked her head out of the carriage's door, a scowl drawing lines across her forehead. "Lady Celia, please come back inside. This is not the thing for young ladies," she called, her gaze narrowing. "You will see us both to ruin."

"Come along, my lady," the coachman urged her to accept a hand up into the conveyance.

Celia stiffened her back and turned her nose up at them. "I shall not cower within the coach and pray for a good outcome. I am responsible for this debacle and I intend to be part of the solution as well." She turned her gaze back to the wheel. The mud encasing it reached halfway up the spokes. Still, she refused to admit defeat. Instead, she picked up her skirts and stepped into the mud. "Perhaps we can push it free?" She said, determination laced through her voice.

She moved to the back of the coach, then placed her hands flush against the boot, allowing the moisture to soak through her gloves and her skirts to rest against the rain-soaked ground.

"My lady!" The coachman exclaimed.

"Lady Celia!" Rosie gasped at nearly the same time as she alighted from the coach.

Two outriders stepped forward, their brows knitted with concern. "Allow us."

The coachman joined them. "Indeed, return to the coach, and we will work to lose the wheel." The coachman stared at her, his gaze imploring.

"Please," Rosie begged, her gaze softening.

Celia released a sigh and stepped back a few feet. "Oh, very well, but we will watch from here. Your work will be easier without the burden of our added weight."

Satisfied, leastwise, for now, the men set about their task.

Rosie came to stand beside Celia, her fingers curled into her cloak, holding it tight about her. "I told you this was a bad idea. In fact, it has become disastrous. The duke will be furious." Rosie shook her head. "I wager he will dismiss me at once."

"Nonsense," Celia pressed her lips together and pulled in a deep breath. "My brother will not hold you accountable for my actions."

After all, he was well acquainted with Celia's antics. She'd wager he would only be furious with her.

Rosie shook her head. "I daresay he will. You have gone too far this time and he will hold me to account—"

"Look." Celia interrupted Rosie's fit, then grinned as the carriage rocked forward, her expression crumbling as it settled back into the mud. "Drat, but I thought they had it dislodged. Surely they almost succeeded." She stepped toward the carriage. "Come help, Rosie. With a bit more strength, we can free the wheel and be on our way. The duke need not know what happened here."

"He'll know. Mark my words, he will." Rosie wrapped her cloak tighter about herself. "You were told to remain in London. The moment you fail to arrive at Lord and Lady Froth's ball, he'll know what you've done."

Celia ignored her companion and joined the men at the back of the carriage. Of course, Charles would learn that she had left London. Celia did not fret about that. What she meant to keep from her brother was the debacle she currently found herself in. He could not scold her as thoroughly if she reached her destination without incident.

The coachman turned his disapproving gaze on her. "My lady, you must not—"

"I'll have none of it," Celia said, her tone brooking no argument. She put her hands flush against the conveyance and ordered, "Push!"

Her heart soared when the coach rocked forward, but it was a short-lived joy as it quickly settled back into the mud. Not to be dissuaded, she said, "Again, with all your strength."

After several attempts, she released a frustrated breath. They needed Rosie's help. Dropping her hands from the coach, she pivoted toward her companion. The mud enveloped her left foot, and she lost her balance. A nearby outrider stopped her descent, but not before her knees met the saturated ground.

"My lady!"

"I am fine. Do not fret," Celia said, allowing him to help her back to her feet. Irritation thick in her voice, Celia peered at Rosie. "Come help, this instant."

To her amazement, Rosie did not protest, and soon the entire group worked to push the coach free of its muddy confines.

Celia's muscles quaked with effort as she braced her feet against the slippery earth and concentrated all of her strength into pushing the coach. "Do not stop," she ordered. "Push."

"What have we here?" A masculine voice interrupted her concentration.

Celia looked toward the newcomer, hoping he would be of help. Her gaze landed on glossy black fur-covered legs. Charles! Her goose was cooked for sure. She squared her shoulders and prepared to defend herself to her brother as she moved her gaze up over the horse's chest and neck to the rider.

Her eyes rounded, then she peered at the man.

The man was not Charles—not even close.

He was broad of shoulder, with deep green eyes

and hair the same inky shade as his horse. She swallowed hard.

Rosie nudged her with her elbow, snapping Celia out of her shocked state.

Celia forced a bright smile. "Good day. I am afraid my coach has gotten stuck in the mud."

"So it would seem." The stranger arched a dark brow. "And you are attempting to push it free?" He continued, amusement dancing in his eyes.

"We nearly succeeded," Celia said, glancing back at the forlorn faces of her servants. "Perhaps you could lend us your strength, Mr...." Her smile grew wider in an attempt to charm the stranger.

He studied the mud-locked wheel for long heartbeats before bursting into laughter.

Furious, Celia turned back to the coach and pushed again. If the scoundrel did not wish to help, then so be it! She did not need him. "Rosie, Herman, Conrad, all of you, help me push." She ordered, but not a one came forward to help.

Instead, a firm hand clamped onto her shoulder. "You are only making it worse. Your horses, and I daresay, your servants, are exhausted."

She spun on the stranger. "You are most vexing, sir. You said you would not help, and yet, you remain. Be on your way if you would be so kind."

"I said I would not help push the coach, for doing so is only digging the wheel deeper into the mud." He waved a hand at the wheel, which was now close to halfway buried in the mud. "I will wager that when you started this fruitless endeavor, it was not so bad?" He arched a questioning brow.

"Listen, Mr…"

"Lord Jasper Crawford," he drawled. "Marquess Crawford, to be exact." He swept into a bow. "And who are you? A lady based on the cut and style of your garments. A milkmaid based on your muddy hem and mussed hair. I must confess that I am intrigued?"

"What you are is intolerable," she seethed even as she noticed how strikingly handsome he was. "I will not allow you to insult me and waste my time. Either lend your help or be on your way."

"Ah, a lady it is." He grinned, his eyes seeming to lighten several shades as he studied her. "I would like to know exactly who I am lending my assistance to." He rocked back on his heels, then added, "If you would be so kind."

Wary of the entire situation, Celia surpassed her frustration and answered, "Very well. I am Lady Celia Kendal, sister to the Duke of Selkirk. Now come help us push." She pivoted back to the coach.

"Not a chance," Lord Crawford said.

Aghast, Celia spun back to him, her finger wagging at him as she yelled, "You scoundrel! You never intended to help. You no good—"

"I have a better way," he said, interrupting her tirade. "A solution that will actually solve your problem."

"Out with it then," she snapped.

"My estate is just up the road. I shall take you there to freshen up and rest, then return with more men, shovels, and fresh horses. Before you know it, your coach will be free, and you will be on your way to…." He narrowed his eyes. "Where are you traveling to?"

"Selkirk Park, my brother's country estate, and I will not be leaving with you," she crossed her arms over her chest. "Not without my companion and outriders."

"So you do have a care for your reputation. How unfortunate, as I am certain we could have a great deal of fun together." He gave a rakish grin, sending a pleasant wave of shivers racing up her spine.

Before she could offer a retort, Lord Crawford turned to her servants and issued a string of orders. To Celia's amazement, they did his bidding, and fast.

Before she knew what had happened, the horses

were untethered, and Rosie was seated before one outrider. The remaining outriders had trunks and valises resting across their thighs. She looked at Lord Crawford, and her mouth went dry. Surely the man did not expect her to ride with him.

"Come along," he said, taking her by the waist and lifting her onto his stallion.

She released an involuntary shriek at his heavy handedness. Celia pressed her lips together to stop herself from protesting further. As vexing as the man was, he could not be expected to walk. Nor could she ask him to act as a servant and haul luggage. If she left her belongings behind, highway men were likely to relieve her of them before anyone returned, and they did not have saddles for the coach horses. Even if they did, the beasts were exhausted.

Celia inhaled a deep breath and notched her chin up, holding her head high.

She could tolerate a brief ride in Lord Crawford's company. Indeed, she could. In fact, she may even enjoy it.

Not his company, for he was a foul man. But the idea of having his body close to hers was not all together unwelcome. After all, he was a prime specimen-broad and strong and handsome. Yes, she rather thought she might enjoy the experience, and so she did not fuss when he mounted behind her and wrapped one muscular arm about her waist.

Celia glanced back at the coach as they rode away. God willing, she would return to it before long. If she could make Yorkshire before Charles returned to London and discover her missing, she would win. Otherwise, he would catch her along the way and force her to return.

Once she made Yorkshire—she would be home, and nothing could force her back to London. Not even her brother, the all powerful duke, could force her hand. She let out a little sigh of contentment.

"Rest," Lord Crawford whispered near her ear.

Liquid fire spread through Celia as she sank against him and closed her eyes. His body pressed to hers, proving to feel every bit as wonderful as she'd suspected it might. Come what may, Charles could never find out about any of this. Agreeing with Rosie that Celia had gone too far this time, he would force Celia to marry or lock her away.

But what Charles did not know could not hurt her.

This would be her secret adventure. Innocent and somehow a little wicked at the same time.

One

Yorkshire, *England*
November, 1819

Mercy, what the devil was he doing here? Celia stared, her mouth agape. She'd never imagined she would see him again—let alone in her family's drawing-room. He was supposed to be a secret—her secret. A long-ago memory never to be faced again. And a bad one at that!

"Collect yourself," Rosie whispered to Celia from behind her fan.

Realizing she was gaping, Celia snapped her mouth shut and inhaled a steadying breath. Her heart pounded against her ribs as she asked, "What is he doing here?"

"You act as if I should know," Rosie replied, her face pale. "It is a house party. Perhaps your brother invited him?" She averted her gaze and whispered, "We may be in trouble."

"I assure you Charles did not invite him. I know all of my brother's friends, and Lord Crawford is not among them," Celia said, her pulse thrumming in her ears. "And neither will we find ourselves in trouble. I will ensure we do not."

"How?" Rosie asked. "The duke may already know everything."

"Impossible, for if he had found out, he'd of already taken me to task." Celia pursed her lips in annoyance. She had to convince Lord Crawford to keep quiet.

His deep green eyes collided with hers, and in another heartbeat, he was heading toward her. Panic gripped her, and her hands shook. She could not allow him to corner her—could not allow for anyone to discover that she knew him.

"Good Lord! It seems he is coming toward us." Rosie stared in his direction, her eyes wide.

Celia spun on her heels and strode for the door. She would not allow him to control this situation. So far as her family knew, Lord Crawford was a stranger. Celia was certain Charles had never discovered the peril she'd placed herself in six months prior, and she did not mean for him to discover it now. Heart pounding, she strode toward the door, hoping Lord Crawford would soon follow.

If she could lure him away from the drawing room, maybe, just maybe, she could convince him to hold his tongue. He was no doubt a scoundrel, but surely he had no wish to face the parson's noose.

Almost there she increased her pace.

"Celia, dear."

A shiver ran through her at Charles's voice, and she froze. Celia plastered a forced smile on to her lips. Double drat! She was cornered. Celia made a slow turn to greet her brother. "Yes, Charles?" She asked sweetly.

"Come meet our guest." Charles glanced toward Lord Crawford while Celia's sister-in-law Julia threaded her arm through Celia's.

Celia did her best to force what she hoped was a welcoming grin as they approached Lord Crawford. She met his gaze. The devil had mischief in his eyes. As much as she did not want to react to him, she could not stop her traitorous body from warming all over. Ignoring the sensations he caused within her, she lifted a prayer that he would follow along with her charade.

She turned her attention to Charles. "I thought all the guests had arrived yesterday."

"All but one. Lord Crawford joined us this afternoon," Charles said, then turned his attention to the marquess. "It is a pleasure to introduce my sister, Lady Celia Kendal."

Celia hesitated for a heartbeat, then said, "It is a pleasure to meet you, my lord." She dipped a customary curtsey, then allowed Lord Crawford to capture her hand. Staring into his eyes, she silently begging him not to reveal their prior acquaintance.

"I feel as though I already know you," he said, amusement dancing in his gaze. He gave a roguish grin, then kissed her hand. "I look forward to becoming better acquainted."

"Indeed, we shall," she said, forcing the words past the tightness in her throat. "If you will excuse me." She gave a quick grin, then pivoted toward the door.

"Where are you going?" Julia asked. "Perhaps I will join you."

Celia had no destination other than away from the drawing room, but she would not confess that fact. Instead, she looked back at Julia, then waved her fan toward the hall and frantically searched her mind for an excuse to leave. "There is no need to accompany me. I simply forgot something in my room. I will be back in a trice. I promise. You should stay and enjoy the guests."

"Very well." Julia nodded.

Celia met Lord Crawford's gaze and tried to convey her thoughts: follow me. She redirected her gaze and strode toward the hall with slow, measured steps. When she reached the threshold, she tossed another glance over her shoulder, first meeting his gaze, then nodding toward the entrance.

She stepped out of the drawing-room to wait a few paces down the corridor. Her heart pounded as the nearby ticking of a clock counted the seconds. Just as she was growing frustrated, Lord Crawford appeared. Celia turned and strode down the hall, her steps much faster this time. Reaching the music room, she stepped inside.

Lord Crawford followed, a grin lighting his deep green eyes. "No need for cat and mouse games, sweeting. A simple invitation would have sufficed."

Celia closed the door and leaned against it. "What are you doing here?" She peered at him.

"I was lured by an ethereal beauty with blond curls and the most captivating blue eyes." He drew closer to her. "A lady who adores mischief and sets my blood on fire."

Celia's cheeks warmed, a mixture of anger and longing fogging up her thoughts. She shook her head. "That is not what I mean, and you well know it."

He pushed a curl back from her cheek. "I'll wager not, but you enjoy the fact that you were able to entice me into following you. The victory has you feeling powerful… desirable."

"Do stop." She swatted his hand away and stepped to the side. "What are you doing at my home? And when will you be leaving?"

"When you caught sight of me in the drawing-room, I saw your eyes light up for a moment before fear darkened their shade. You were happy to see me." He leaned against the piano. "Go on, deny it."

"I… This is ridiculous." She heaved a sigh and took several steps back. "I was surprised to find you in my home. Nothing more."

He closed the distance between them. Caught her in his arms and pulled her against him. "You were elated."

Her blood turned molten, her heart beating rapidly. "I was not," she lied, though she did not attempt to leave his embrace.

"Tell me you have not thought of me since that day?" He stared into her eyes, searching.

Celia swallowed hard, memories of their time together scrolling through her mind. The way he had kissed her. The way her body had come alive in his arms. She'd wanted him then. She wanted him now. She bit her lip—hard. "I have not." The fallacy slid off her tongue.

"Lier," he whispered against her lips before pressing his mouth to hers.

She gave no resistance, her arms coming up to encircle his neck as their mouths melded together, hot and wet and hungry. Her entire body thrummed with desire as he kissed her, deep and hard—as she kissed him back. A small moan tore from deep within her.

He pulled his mouth from hers, smiled a roguish grin. "You missed me."

"Very well, I missed you. However, that does not mean that I am happy to see you." She moved her arms back to her sides. "In fact, I am the exact opposite of happy."

"You wound me." He said, a feigned look of hurt altering his expression. "And after I went to so much trouble."

She smirked up at him. "Tell me about that. How is it you have come to be here? In my home."

He nuzzled his face into her hair and said, "If you insist."

"I do." She stiffened her back and stepped from his embrace.

He released her and scrubbed his hand over his jaw. "I made a rather substantial donation to the Duchess's home for women. The sort that is too large to ignore."

"Scoundrel," Celia swatted his arm.

"I have never denied the fact." He caught her by the waist. "And you like that about me."

"I most certainly do not." She tried to look indignant. "I am a lady, Lord Crawford." Old anger swarmed through her. Anger she thought she'd thought she left in the past.

"Believe me when I say I am all too aware of the fact." He drew nearer.

She placed the palms of her hands against his hard, muscled chest. "Then why, pray tell, are you here?" If he took her back in his arms, she doubted her ability to resist. It had taken everything in her to deny herself—to deny them both that day. She simply did not have it in her to do it again.

"I could not stop thinking about you. It is the

damndest thing, but I cannot get you out of my mind." He stroked a finger across her jaw. "I had to see you again."

She pulled away from his touch even as she wanted to lean in. "And now that you have?" Celia asked.

His green eyes smoldered as he caught her wrist and brought her arm around his neck. "I intend to taste you again."

Her resistance crumbled. Celia thought she would incinerate as his mouth took hers, his tongue plundering and claiming. Then all thoughts save for one fled her mind—she wanted him.

Two

J asper Knoll, the fifth Marquess of Crawford, had gone to a great deal of trouble to see Lady Kendal. After spending months with memories of her racing through his mind, he'd donated a king's ransom to the Duchesses charity house.

More over, he'd done so in person, and to his surprise, the Duchess had thanked him with an invitation to her house party.

He had thought that seeing Lady Kendal—blast it, seeing Celia again—would free him of his longing for her. Jasper had been intimate with enough women to know that the second kiss was never as exhilarating as the first.

And yet, the second time he kissed her, more than passion stirred.

His very soul took notice. His heart. His entire mind and body.

It was for that reason he took her mouth a third time. As he held her close, their hearts beating in perfect rhythm while their mouths worked together, he knew he had to have her. All of her—forever.

With great reluctance, Jasper broke their kiss, but he could not bring himself to release his hold on her. He did not wish to. This was more than infatuation. More than mere lust. What he felt for her… It was more than he believed possible.

She stared up at him, her blue eyes smoky and cheeks flushed with passion.

"Marry me," he demanded.

"What?" Confusion clouded her gaze.

He brought his face closer to hers and inhaled her scent of jasmine and vanilla. "I asked you to marry me."

She laughed, an awkward and confused cacophony.

"I am quite serious, Celia. Lady Kendal." He pulled her closer, bringing her body flush against his. "Become my marchioness."

"You have gone quite mad," she said, then stepped

from his embrace. "This…" She shook her head. "Whatever is between us…." She averted her gaze. "You are mad."

"Mad with the need to have you at my side." He reached for her, but she dodged his attempt. "Celia, I am completely insane with the need to have you. To hold and keep you. I want to possess you, to feel your skin against mine and hear your sighs and moans filling my bed-chamber. But that is not the half of it. I want to protect and spoil you. To see you across the dining table and dance with you at balls. I want to raise children with you and grow old beside you."

She placed her hand on his forehead. "Are you ill?" Her brow knit in worry.

"I assure you I am not unwell."

"Then you must be foxed," she retorted. "You scarcely know me and you are proposing marriage. And after—"

He cut off her tirade, asking, "Did you taste whiskey in my kiss?"

Her cheeks turned the most becoming shade of scarlet at his question, and Jasper could scarcely stop himself from pulling her back into his arms. Somehow, he controlled himself, but only because he did not want to frighten her. He realized his declarations had come too fast.

"I daresay I do not believe your declarations and have no intentions of playing whatever game you are about." She turned up her pert little nose and pressed her lips together.

"I am not ill, neither am I in my cups. What I am is enamored with you, Lady Kendal. This is no game, and I intend to prove it. I will not stop pursuing you until you marry me. Hell, even then I will not stop. I will woo you until the day I die."

She blew out a frustrated breath. "I am returning to the drawing-room. I suggest you take your leave before the rain moves in." She pivoted, then disappeared into the hallway.

Jasper could not help but find encouragement in the challenge that laced through her tone and the glint in her eyes. She acted perturbed, but he could see through her facade.

She wanted him to pursue her, and he would not disappoint. 'A lady needs more than one night of passion. They long for a lifetime.' Her words came back to him on a memory. He had treated her badly then, and now he meant to make up for it. Jasper would give her what she desired. He'd win her heart and take her to wife before the new year dawned.

Stepping around the piano, he moved to the side-board, then poured two fingers of brandy. It would be a fine way to pass ten minutes before returning to the drawing-room.

Besides, her kisses had him quite undone. He was not at all fit for society in his present state. A bit of time to get his emotions under control would serve him well.

Sipping from the brandy, Jasper leaned against the sideboard and considered his next move. Perhaps he should launch his own game of hard to get. Ignore her until she came running to him.

He swirled the liquor in his glass as he dismissed the idea. She was impossible to ignore. Trying to do so would prove a fool's errand. Besides, she was as stubborn as a mule and as feisty as a hornet trapped in a bonnet. No matter how badly she wanted to come to him, she would resist.

Because he had given her every reason to doubt him.

He had to show her he was serious and that she could trust him. And he needed her cooperation to do so. Celia had to be wooed and charmed. He would need to build on their previous connection and prove that he wanted more than her body. He had to become her friend. They had started off on a poorly six months prior but quickly plunged into a camaraderie before he went and ruined what was transpiring between them.

They could do so again. He could regain her respect and so much more along the way.

With his path chosen, Jasper finished his drink, then strode toward the drawing-room. Song greeted him as he drew nearer. A single female voice—Celia's. He stepped into the room, his gaze finding hers.

"O weep not, sweet maid, nor let sorrow oppress thee,...." Her eyes sparkled as she sang the haunting words, her breasts rising and falling with her breaths while she pressed one hand flat against her trim midsection. She looked like an ethereal seductress, and he was in want of seduction.

Jasper's gaze moved to her plump, bow-shaped lips. They were like ripe berries and tasted even sweeter. He pulled his gaze from her. The woman was driving him to distraction without even trying.

"And angels will pity such beauty in tears...."

As she continued to sing, he moved to the refreshment table and retrieved a glass of punch. He took a long drink, all the while wishing he had his flask. As she finish the performance, he picked up another glass of punch, then strode toward her. "You must be thirsty," he said, offering the glass.

She grinned, accepting the offering. "That was thoughtful," she said before taking a slow drink of the sweet punch. She swallowed, then lowered the glass, an impish grin curving her lips. "May I ask why you are still here?"

He chuckled, the heaviness in his heart dissipating at the way her lush lips curved and eyes sparkled. "You are smiling because you are glad I have not gone."

"I daresay you see right through me. Still, I must point out that nothing will come of your remaining." She took another sip of the punch he'd given her. "I am a lady."

"In my experience, ladies often take husbands." He smoothed his cravat as he held her gaze. "You told me you intend to marry."

"Yes, but you are not the marrying type." She shook her head, the blond curls piled atop her head bounced with the movement. "You said as much when we last met."

"I was a fool," he said. Jasper stepped closer and offered his arm. "And I intend to prove it to you."

She accepted his offer, her hand resting on his

elbow. "Now that sounds promising. Tell me what exactly you intend to do?"

"I am going to court you," he said matter-of-factly, "then I am going to marry you."

Celia shook her head. "You jest." She laughed.

"Not in the least, Lady Kendal." He placed his hand over hers where it rested on his arm, then met her gaze. "Welcome me to stay and allow me to court you."

Her steps faltered. "If I agree, will you promise to keep our past meeting a secret?"

He stilled so she could gain her balance. "You little hypocrite, you want me here? You are just afraid of being found out." His grin broadening at the chagrin in her expression. "I would never invite scandal on my future wife."

"Then you have leave to stay." Her eyes lightened as she flipped her fan open and brought it up to shade her face. "And you may court me with kisses."

"Minx," he said in playful reprimand.

Three

$\sim$

Celia knew who the letter was from before she opened it, and her heart delighted with the knowledge. She unfolded the parchment with all the joy of a child on Christmastide, then read his words.

Meet me in the conservatory.
JC

Celia pressed the note to her breasts. She could scarcely believe Lord Crawford was in her home. Even more unfathomable, he wished to court her. There had been many times since she left his estate that she'd hoped for this very thing.

Though she'd never dared to believe it could

happen. He had been adamant about avoiding marriage, and she had been adamant about settling for nothing less. When she departed his home, she did so with great regret and sorrow—as well as a healthy dose of anger toward the scoundrel. Celia had been certain they had no future. She'd been equally certain that she would never see him again.

Their passionate encounter had ended with a declaration that nothing more would ever happen between them. She would not squander her virtue and he would not relinquish his bachelor status. They had gone from passionate caresses and searing kisses to angry words and insults.

Yet, here he was, writing her notes and kissing her without attempting to bed her. Could he truly wish to marry her? Or was it all a design to get under her skirts? She blew out a deep breath, then dropped the letter into her sliver trinket box and closed the lid. There was but one way to discover his true intentions.

She had to let him court her. Had to allow him a chance to prove his intentions. She only prayed that her heart could handle breaking yet again if he proved to be the scoundrel of the past rather than the honorable man he was now presenting to her.

But did she not owe it to herself to find out?

Celia took a moment to pinch her cheeks and smooth her coiffure, then quit her bedchamber. Her pulse thrummed, and her hands shook as she traversed the corridors leading to the conservatory. She fretted about his sincerity and turned back more than once before reaching the conservatory. Ultimately, she pressed onward as if pulled by an invisible thread.

Jasper was here. He had come for her.

All of her nerves dissipated when she caught sight of him standing outside of the conservatory door, waiting for her. Lord, he was handsome, and that grin—it curled her toes.

Celia watched Jasper's expression as he led her into the conservatory. There was a joy about him, much like the wonder that danced in a child's eyes when they discovered something new. Could it be that he had discovered love?

Certainly not, she scolded herself. They scarcely knew each other. But perhaps he liked her enough to consider the idea. Indeed, he must if he intended to marry her. She fanned herself, the silk ribbons of her hand-painted fan dancing from the efforts.

The conservatory was one of her favorite places. Celia loved the colors and smells of the many plants and flowers. She and Julia tended to some of the plants grown within the room. Many of the vases in the house held flowers they had tended. With Charles's consent, they had even installed a fountain and benches next to the stream that cut across the conservatory.

She and Julia passed many an afternoon sitting there as they trimmed plants or removed thorns from roses. Sometimes they simply sat enjoying the scents and sounds of the conservatory. They recently had an evergreen tree brought in and potted near the stream. Much to her brother's amusement, they already decorated it for Christmastide.

Charles had teased them mercifully, saying it was far too early to do such a thing, but she and Julia cared not. They did it anyway. Julia defended them by pointing out that Christmastide was but a few of weeks off.

Celia turned a speculative gaze on Lord Crawford as the tree came into view. "Does your family decorate trees for the holiday?"

"I see no reason to decorate at all," he answered.

"How unfortunate," she said, giving his arm a slight squeeze. "How does one celebrate Christmastide without decorating?"

"They do not." He brought them to a stop in front

of the evergreen. "I see no point in celebrating when there is no one to share it with."

"But what of your sister? Could you not celebrate with her?" Celia asked, her heart hurting for him.

"She disapproves of my lifestyle. We have not seen each other for many years. Not since she married." Lord Crawford reached out and ran a fingertip over the petals of a red paper rose.

"I made that one," she said, a heaviness setting into her heart.

He grinned. "It is lovely. I am not surprised to discover you crafted it."

"Could you not celebrate with your servants? You are a Marquess. What about celebrating for the sake of your tenants?"

He turned his attention to the babbling stream. "I give generously to those under my care. There have been no complaints."

Celia closed her fan. "I imagine not, but I also think they would enjoy a celebration."

He turned to her. "They have their own families and friends. I have been content with my lot."

"Still, the thought of you alone at Christmas pains me."

"It should not, for it has been my choice." He led her away from the tree and toward the fountain.

Celia's brow furrowed with concern. "I find it a terrible choice."

"Then you should be pleased to have me celebrating with you this Christmastide." He winked.

"You seem a bit too confident in that assumption. Christmastide is still several months away." She turned her gaze back to him. "I cannot do anything about Christmastide, but I assure you, I am most pleased you choose to stay for now." In one bold move, she placed her hand on his cravat. "And I dare say you will choose to celebrate if I become your wife."

His grin turned seductive, his gaze burning into hers as he brought his mouth close to hers. "I will if I have you at my side."

Celia angled her chin to welcome his kiss. When he did not close the scant distance remaining, she batted her lashes in confusion. "Are you not going to kiss me?" She asked.

He trailed his finger across her lips. "I believe you have been kissed enough."

Her cheeks burned, indignation lighting within her. "That is a fine thing to say. And here I thought we were getting on well." She pivoted and strode toward the glass door leading into the side yard.

"Wait. I admit, that was poorly done. Allow me to explain," he called after her.

She stopped and crossed her arms over her breasts. One foot tapped impatiently. "Go on."

"What I should have said is that I want us to form a deeper bond. I do not want to seduce you. I want to come to know you fully. To forge a friendship."

Her heart fluttered at the words. "You expect me to believe that?"

He cringed, his mouth pressing into a tight line and brow furrowing. "You make me sound like such a cad," he said, hurt in his tone.

Celia had every reason to distrust him. Every reason to doubt him. Least he'd forgotten, she said, "Let us not forget our first meeting, Lord Crawford." She pointed at him. "You were quite clear about your desires and intentions then, so excuse me if I do not trust you now."

"My actions were inexcusable. Intolerable, even, and you have every right to exercise caution." He stepped closer and captured her hands in his. "It is the very reason I will not kiss you. I will do nothing that a gentleman would not do. You have my word, Celia. I will earn your respect, friendship, and ultimately, your heart."

He pressed his lips to her gloved knuckles, first the right hand, then the left.

The act nearly undid her. She wanted to give herself over to him. To believe every word he spoke and embrace the future he offered.

Still, she hesitated.

He seemed very different, but could a man change so much in a matter of months? Could she have had such an effect on him in such a short amount of time? Celia could not help but guard her heart. She stared deep into his eyes and asked, "Why?" Her throat tightened even as she spoke.

"Because I want a lifetime with you. The words you spoke to me... The way you dominate my thoughts and dreams. I cannot explain it, but I know I need you in my life. Give me a chance, Celia."

She nodded. "Know that if you are toying with me, I will see you punished."

He smiled and held out his hand. "Dance with me, Celia?"

She accepted his offer and allowed him to pull her close. Rather than point out the obvious, she hummed a waltz.

He led her through the dance, their movements in perfect sync. Bringing his mouth close to her ear, he said, "We dance together as if we have done so a million times before."

His breath on her ear caused a riot of sensations within her, and yet, it was his statement that affected her the most. Celia admitted the truth to herself. She'd danced hundreds of times with dozens of partners, but never had it come so naturally.

There was something between them. Something real. Perhaps they had a future together. Maybe they were made for one another. The spark of hope she'd held near as she made her way to the conservatory ignited into a full-blown fire, and she prayed Jasper had come to her in earnest. Prayed there was indeed a future for them to share.

He pressed her close as they danced around a bend in the cobblestone path.

She gave a saucy smile. "I wonder what else we do well together?"

"Temptress," he growled.

Her laughter filled the conservatory.

Four

C andlelight filled the room as stemware clinked and silverware clattered. The Duke and Duchess's guests conversed and laughed as they dined. To Jasper's displeasure, he had not been seated near Celia. Instead, he was across the table and several chairs down with the dowager countess Grayling and Miss Harrington flanking him. The first was a stern old woman who did nothing to hide her distaste for him, and the second was a mousey young chit who could not bring herself to partake in conversation.

The fact suited him fine, as he only had eyes for Celia. Though he wished to seated close enough to engage with her, watching her was second best. Given his dinner companions' aversions, he would not be distracted from watching her. And watch her, he did. Every time she lifted her glass to her lips, he wished he could kiss them. Every smile she bestowed on her companions sent a pang of jealousy through him. And every time she laughed, he wished he'd been the catalyst for her joy.

It was a foreign sensation, one he had rarely, if ever, felt before. In fact, he did not recognize it for jealousy until he had experienced it several times. But what other emotion could make a man want to pummel another simply because a woman smiled at him?

Her gaze meet his, and her tongue darted out to wet her lower lip. His body reacted immediately, tightening all over as his pulse increased. Based on the wicked grin she shot him, the minx was well aware of what she had done. The sensual game lasted throughout the rest of the meal.

When she left the dining room with the ladies, she tossed a saucy glance his way before disappearing into the hall. The preceding hour he spent smoking cigars and drinking brandy with the men felt like an eternity. Talk of crops and tenant farmers could not compete with his desire to get Celia alone.

Grateful to be rejoining the ladies, Jasper strode into the parlor. His gaze searched for Celia, and heart rejoiced when he found her. She stood near a window chatting like a magpie with a group of ladies. Content to watch her for the time being, Jasper leaned against a marble column flanking the wall. He could spend the rest of his life observing her.

"Lord Crawford."

He turned his attention to the speaker, then straightened and offered a bow. "Your Grace."

"I had hoped to thank you again for your donation, but now I am more interested in your intentions." The Duchess seemed to assess him as she searched his face.

"Hum." Jasper cleared his throat. "My intentions?"

The duchess angled her head toward Celia. "I could not help but notice the way you and my sister-in-law carried on during dinner. And now, well, you have been staring at her since you entered the parlor."

He smoothed his cravat, thinking he should be embarrassed, or at the least chagrined at being caught. But he did not care to pretend. Instead, he smiled, then said, "I find her captivating."

"She is a beautiful girl. I daresay, a diamond," The Duchess said.

"She is, but I am interested in more than her beauty," Jasper said.

"That is reassuring." The duchess pointed her fan toward her husband. "I would be remiss if I did not tell you how protective the duke is of his sister. Tread carefully."

Jasper did not miss the warning in her gaze. But neither did he care. He would die a thousand deaths if it meant he got to spend one more second in Celia's company. Still, he would not dare insult the duchess, so he said, "My intentions are honorable. You have my word."

"Very good." She nodded, then pivoted and strode away.

Jasper returned his gaze to Celia. The group of ladies had dispersed, leaving her with only her companion at her side. He strode toward her. "Good evening, ladies."

"Good evening, Lord Crawford," Rosie said, then pressed her lips together, casting her gaze to Celia.

The woman's disapproval did not bother him. He knew it was born of the high regard she held for Celia. That and the knowledge she had of the time they had spent together. He would leave it to Celia to manage her companion.

"Please excuse us," Celia said to her.

The woman gave a slight "hump" then went to sit on a nearby sofa, her attention trained on them.

"She detests me," Jasper said.

Celia shook her head. "Certainly not."

"You are a terrible liar."

"Very well. She dislikes you, but surely you did not come over here to speak of my companion's feelings." Celia turned, her gaze moving to the window and the snow-covered ground that lay beyond. "Do you like the snow?"

"I have never thought too much about it. The stuff makes a devil of a mess, and it is cold. Still, there is a beauty about it when it falls. A peacefulness to it when it blankets the ground."

Celia turned a wistful grin on him. "As a girl, I used to love to run through freshly fallen snow, and I could spend hours staring at a set of tracks left by one animal or another."

"I used to make a game of following the tracks," he admitted. Jasper turned his attention back to the snow-covered ground. "Let us go out and see if we can find a set."

Excitement lit her blue gaze. "I will meet you behind the house in thirty minutes."

Forty minutes later, Jasper stood outside in the freshly fallen snow, his greatcoat blocking the cold.

To his surprise, there was no wind. Just still air between the glistening snow and sparkling sky. It was a perfect night save for one thing. Celia had yet to arrive. He turned to glance at the house, wondering if she had changed her mind.

Thwack!

Something crashed into his shoulder. He turned in time to see a snowball soaring through the air.

Thwack!

It exploded into a powdery cloud against his chest. His gaze followed the sound of feminine laughter that rang out nearby. "Minx," he yelled when he caught sight of Celia forming another ball.

He bent and scooped up a handful of snow. Two could play this game. As he took aim, her snowball struck him in the abdomen. Laughter filled the night air as she danced away, ducking behind a tree.

Jasper let his snowball fall to the ground and ran toward her hiding spot. He charged across the space, ducking and weaving through her assault of round white missiles. When he reached her, he wrapped his arm around her and tugged her against him, so they stood chest to chest.

She notched her chin. Her gaze turning sultry. "Will you kiss me now?"

He shook his head. "Not unless you have accepted my proposal."

She brought her hand up and rubbed the snow she held against his face. Shocked at her antics, he released her, and she bolted. Celia laughed as she ran breakneck across the snow.

He found her vivacious personality contagious, as he, too, laughed. Moments before he caught her, she stopped and said, "Look."

He did not have time to stop and instead crashed into her, sending them both to the ground. She landed with her head against his chest and a cloak wrapped around their legs. He pulled her close and asked, "Are you hurt?"

"No." She nibbled at her lower lip and looked up at the inky black sky. "I saw a shooting star."

"Oh?" He asked, his hand coming up to stroke her cheek.

"Do you know what they say about shooting stars?" She asked as she rolled onto her back.

"That someone has passed onto their last reward."

"That is dreadful and not at all what they say."

It did not surprise him in the least that she would have an entirely different idea. He smiled, his arm still beneath her head, and said, "Enlighten me."

"Papa used to say that every time a star shoots across the sky, someone has fallen in love." Her voice took on a wistful tone laced with sadness.

Jasper rolled onto his side and stared into her eyes. "How old were you when you lost your parents?"

"Fifteen," she replied. "How old were you?"

"Nineteen."

Celia sighed, then asked, "Do you miss them very much?"

"It gets better with time, but I still think of them far too often." He settled back into the snow, holding her close. "Tell me about your parents."

He listened intently as she spoke of her childhood and her memories. Then he returned the favor by telling her about his. Seconds passed into minutes, and when he felt her shiver, he realized he had lost all sense of time. "You are chilled through. Let us get you inside."

"I'm perfectly comfortable."

He trailed his gaze over her red cheeks and blue lips. "Lier," he teased as he stood, then helped her to her feet.

"You could warm me with a kiss." She stared at him from beneath a veil of thick lashes.

"Not until you agree to marry me."

"We could compromise," she said, pressing closer against him.

His entire body thrummed with the need to possess her, and he nearly caved to the temptation. His lips pressed against hers, and if not for the icy feel of her flesh, he would have succumbed. Instead, he scooped her into his arms and made haste for the house.

Five

Celia snuggled into her bed, pulling her blankets up to her chest as she reveled in the evening's magic. She had long held a tender for the first snow of the season, but had never enjoyed so thoroughly before. Despite the cold, she would have remained outdoors all night so long as Jasper was at her side.

Rosie had seen to it she had a warm bath and hot tea when she returned to the house, but it was thoughts of Jasper that truly warmed Celia. She simply could not stop thinking about him and the possibility of a future together.

She turned to Rosie, who sat nearby, fretting. "There really is no reason for you to stay with me."

Rosie turned an incredulous stare on her.

"Someone has to watch for a fever. You may have caught your death."

Celia waved a hand dismissively. "Do not be so dramatic, Rosie."

"You came in frozen to the marrow. Far less has caused a fever. I am scarcely being dramatic," Rosie said. "And shame Lord Crawford for allowing it," she added.

Celia pushed her covers back and swung her legs over the side of her bed.

"What are you about now?" Rosie asked, her brow furrowed.

Celia slid from the bed and started toward her private sitting room. "I need to write Lord Crawford a letter."

Rosie stood and followed Celia. "What you need to do is rest."

"Rubbish." Celia said, dismissing the idea. "I am perfectly well and shall remain as such." She ignored the rest of Rosie's protests and settled into the chair at her writing desk before taking a quill in hand.

I have been sufficiently thawed.
CK

Celia folded the scrap of parchment and held it

out to Rosie. "Go slip this under Lord Crawford's door."

"I most certainly will not." Rosie crossed her arms over her bosom.

Celia heaved a long-suffering sigh. "Very well, I will do it myself." She pulled her wrapper tight and strode toward the door.

Rosie raced to get in front of her. "Stubborn girl. Give it to me. You cannot go trapping about the house in your nightclothes during a house party. It seems you are determined to ruin yourself. I will not allow it."

Celia held the note close to her body. "Everyone is abed. No one will see me."

Rosie held out her hand. "I will deliver it," she said, exasperation in her tone.

Celia grinned with victory, then said, "Thank you, Rosie."

She held the note out, and Rosie took it, then stepped into the hall. She turned back to Celia and said, "I expect to find you in bed when I return."

"If I am in bed, will you agree to retire to your own room so that I may rest without your gaze upon me?" Celia asked hopefully. "It is rather disconcerting to be watched so closely."

"I will bring you some fresh tea," Rosie replied before striding down the hall.

Celia returned to her bed, but she had no hope of sleeping. Her mind was far too occupied with thoughts and memories. Before long, Rosie returned with the promised tea. Celia accepted a cup and sipped from it as she considered how she might get Rosie to leave her alone. Before long, her thoughts returned to Jasper.

"Did Lord Crawford get the note?"

Rosie looked up from the book she was reading. "I suspect so. I slipped it beneath his door as you requested." She narrowed her gaze at Celia. "How is it you have gone from despising the man to writing him clandestine letters?"

"There was nothing clandestine about it," Celia said.

Rosie closed her book with a thud. "All of this time, I thought you held a grudge because the Marquess poked fun at you when the coach was stuck. Now I think far more transpired between the two of you. What exactly happened last spring? And why have you forgiven him now?"

Celia pressed her lips together and sank back against her pillows.

"If you tell me, I will retire to my room and let you sleep without my fussing over you."

Celia could not refuse Rosie's offer. She pinned her gaze to the ceiling and considered where to start. "Do you believe in love at first sight?"

"I believe in attraction at first sight," Rosie replied.

"No." Celia shook her head. "Attraction is different. That is animalistic and easy to satisfy. I am talking about something much more profound. The desire to be near someone, to delight in the smallest attentions and have your heart squeeze with pain when they are not near. The simple joy in having them close and deep satisfaction in the simplest of touches. An undeniable pull toward another soul." Celia blew out a breath. "A connection that seems to exist for no reason at all, but is there non-the-less."

"Are you trying to tell me you are in love with Lord Crawford?"

"Perhaps, but that is not what I was trying to say."

"Then I must confess to being confused." Rosie leaned forward and propped her chin on her fists. "What were you trying to convey?"

"That day last spring, I remember thinking Lord Crawford was the most handsome man I had ever seen. But it was more than that. I felt a pull toward him. A connection, unlike anything I could have imagined before."

Rosie huffed a breath. "You could have fooled me."

"That was the point," Celia said. "It startled me. I choose to ignore it and cover the feelings with anger instead. I was so frustrated, and he did not help with his contradictory words and then the way he took charge, and all of you did exactly as he commanded. It was easy to allow my vexation to cover what I was feeling."

Celia turned when she heard the shuffle of feet outside the door. Her heart somersaulted when she saw a letter slide into her chamber.

"Stay in bed." Rosie held up her hand as she stood from the chair to retrieve the note.

Celia's heart pounded while she waited for Rosie to give her the parchment. The moment Celia's fingers closed on the carefully folded square, she opened it. Then grinned at the words scribbled on the parchment.

I should like to see for myself.
JC

"What does it say?"

Celia's smile grew, warmth spreading through her. "Nothing important."

"I very much doubt that." Rosie settled back into the chair. "But at the moment, I am more interested in the past. I cannot imagine that you came to detest Lord Crawford simply because you were drawn to him."

"Indeed, not." Celia tucked the note behind her pillow and continued with the tale. "It was after we dinned and you went above stairs to rest. I joined Lord Crawford in the parlor for a game of cards. We were having a fine time of it, talking and jesting. We grew tired of the game and went to sit by the hearth."

"You should have gone to bed," Rosie mused.

"He kissed me." Celia felt her cheeks warm at the confession.

"He what?" Rosie turned wide eyes on Celia. "Are you ruined? There will be hell to pay when the duke learns of this. That is why the color drained from your face when you saw him again. We have to—"

"Stop." Celia held out her hand, palm first. "I am not ruined. We kissed, and a little more, but when he hiked up my skirts, I stopped him."

"Thank the good lord!" Rosie exclaimed. "Then what?"

"Then I told him I was a lady and would not lose my virtue outside of the marriage bed." She sighed. "He stood and strode across the room before turning back to me and announcing that he would never marry. I scolded him, called him a rogue and a scoundrel, and told him he was unfit for my presence or that of any other lady. I said other things, and so did he, but they are too terrible to repeat. Regardless, I was glad he did not bother to wave us off, and never planned to see him again."

"Good for you," Rosie said. "But now? Why is he here?" Her voice rose as she went on. "Why are you welcoming him?"

Celia turned onto her side and cuddled her extra pillow. "Now, he is completely different. He has proposed to me multiple times and refuses to kiss me. He insists he made a mistake and wants me at his side."

Rosie leaned forward and took Celia's hand. "That is a comfort, but surely you do not trust him."

"I did not. I was furious to discover Lord Crawford here." Celia got out of bed again and went back to her desk. "I even told him to leave, but he refused and insisted on getting to know me better. He wishes to court me properly." She turned to Rosie. "I am glad of it because now I know he cares for me. I suspect he felt the same bond that I did when we met. It has to be love, Rosie. What else could it be?"

"Madness," Rosie said, shaking her head. "You scarcely know him."

"I know enough." Celia smiled. "I know he sought a way to find me. That he donated a substantial sum of money to Julia's charity to get an invitation to the house party. I know he has refused to kiss me despite my invitations. And I know he has asked me to marry him more than once." She turned back to her desk and crafted her reply.

Then she held the parchment out to Rosie. "I know he makes me laugh and has a strange way of seeing right through me. He understands me and enjoys my mischief. And I know his kisses light me on fire. I am going to marry him."

Rosie took the letter. "I hope you do not come to regret your choice."

Celia squeezed Rosie's hand around the letter. "One cannot go wrong when they follow their heart."

Six

J asper saw the letter as it slipped into his bedchamber and made his way to the door before it lost its momentum. He picked up the square of parchment and unfolded the letter.

I accept. I will become your marchioness.
CK

Jasper read the words scrolled in Celia's feminine handwriting. His heart elated at the simple words—I accept. Squeezing the letter in his hand, he started toward his desk to reply, then turned toward the door. The hell with writing. He wanted to hold her close. See the warmth in her eyes and feel the softness of her lips.

She would marry him. He would spend the rest of his life with her at his side. They would build a future—a family.

Celia forgave him. She trusted him, and she wanted him.

With long, quick strides, he made his way to her room.

She was waiting for him with her hip resting against the doorjamb. "I knew you would come to me," she said, a satisfied grin playing at her lips.

"I will always come to you," he took a step closer. "Say it out loud, Celia. Tell me you meant what you wrote. Say you will marry me."

She backed into her room, stepping to the side in order to allow him entrance.

He followed, his gaze never wandering from hers.

She shut the door, then reached for him. "I will marry you."

He swept her into his arms and held her tight against his pounding heart. "You will not regret this, Celia. I swear to you, I will make you happy. I will treasure you and honor you until I draw my last breath."

"I already regret my choice."

"What?" He loosed his hold on her and stared down at her. Much to his relief, there was playfulness in her gaze. "What reason do you have for regret so soon?"

She wet her lips. "You have yet to kiss me." She rose on to her toes, bringing her lips closer to his. "I shall want lots of kisses. Dozens each day and every night before I fall to sleep, too."

"Then you shall have them." Jasper covered her mouth with his. Every ounce of love and longing he felt went into the kiss. He thrust his tongue into her mouth, claiming and branding her. Passion and tenderness flowed through him and she meet his demand with one all her own. By the time he pulled away, they were both breathless.

"Are you satisfied now?" He teased.

"Humm… Not quite," she said, her voice full of mischief. "When will you bed me?" A slight blush painted her cheeks as she spoke.

"The moment we are wed," he replied. Which meant to blasted long in his estimation, but he wanted to do this right. He had to show her the respect she deserved. Had to honor what they shared. "I will need to procure a license. Unless you wish for the banns to be read."

"Three weeks. I do not think I could stand the wait." Her grin grew wider, her gaze soft and sparkling. "I should like to marry this very night."

He pressed a kiss to the top of her head. "I would give you anything, but marring tonight is beyond my power."

"Lucky for you, I have some power of my own." She twirled her finger in the hair at the back of his neck. "My brother is a duke, after all. One who believes in the necessity of being prepared for any circumstance that might arise."

Jasper chuckled, then kissed her again. "I suppose having an unwed sister would necessitate the need for a handy license?"

"Most certainly." She backed toward the door; bring him with her. "Go dress. I will have someone wake the duke and duchess."

"My valet can fetch the vicar," Jasper said as he stole one last kiss before departing.

Two hours later, Celia was introduced as the Marchioness of Crawford amid a round of cheers. Charles and Julia had awakened the entire party to come and watch the nuptials take place, after which they all moved to the ballroom.

Jasper handed her a glass of champagne. "Are you pleased?"

"Very much so," she said as she looked across the room to where Julia and Charles danced. "I could not ask for more."

"Are you certain?"

She nodded, then took a sip of the bubbly drink.

"Dance with me." He took her glass and set it on a passing servant's tray.

Celia laughed as he swept her onto the dance floor, then held her scandalously close.

He whispered in her ear, "I love you."

She stopped dancing, tears pricking at her eyes. "I never… I did not dare dream… Not so soon."

He caught her chin between his thumb and forefinger and stared deep into her eyes. "I love you. I have loved you from the moment I set eyes on you clad in your muddy frock. And I will love you for eternity."

"Oh, Jasper." She pressed her lips to his. "I love you too. Take me to bed now. I long to be your wife in every way."

"Are you sure?" He asked, not wanting to rush her. "I will wait until you are ready. Hours, days, or years, I will wait."

"I do not want to wait another second." She took his hand and tugged him toward the door.

He could barely continence that this beautiful

woman was his wife. That he alone would get to hold her and love her for the rest of his days. And he, too, wanted to solidify the vows they had spoken.

When they reached their room, he tumbled her onto the bed, then covered her body with his. His mouth taking hers in a hungry, demanding kiss. Their tongues thrusting together as the wet heat of her mouth infused his.

She tugged and pulled at his clothing until she worked her hands inside of his shirt. "I want to feel you. Take it off," she said, her words husky, demanding.

"As you wish, wife." Jasper moved off her long enough to discard his waistcoat, cravat, and shirt. He ran a finger across her décolletage. "I wish to touch you." He helped her sit, then trailed kisses down her throat, across her collarbone, and over her shoulder as he undid the buttons running down her back.

She moaned and wiggled, pushing her gown down to her waist. Her hands trailed over his shoulders and down his back as he bent his head to her breasts, kissing each mound before pulling one pink nipple into his mouth and suckling.

Her back arched as she cried out for more, her fingers tangled in his hair. "I want you. I want all of you, Jasper."

He wanted to be deep within her, too, but knew she was not ready. Releasing her nipple, he said, "Be patient, love. I do not want to hurt you."

She reached for the buttons of his falls. "You won't," she said.

He rolled onto his back and let her do as she pleased. When his cock sprang free of its confines, she reached for it. Her fingers feathering tentatively over his length. His body jerked in response. Then she curled her fingers around his cock, and a guttural moan tore from deep within him.

"You like that?" She asked, her gaze full of wonder.

He thrust into her hand. "You make me wild with desire."

"Show me how to please you," she said, her gaze locked with his.

She smiled as he brought his hand over hers and guided her movements. The action nearly undid him, and he stilled her hand, moving it away from his cock. "Now it is my turn to please you," he said, guiding her to lie back.

In another minute, he was kissing her, his fingers creeping up past her silk stockings to play with the downy curls between her thighs. "Relax and allow me to worship you."

Her lips parted as her thighs opened.

He kissed his way down her body, starting at her lips and making his way to her waist. She reached for her gown and helped him drag it down her legs. He kissed his way back up her legs, teasing the back of her knees before continuing up her inner thighs.

Celia tangled her fingers in his hair and panted as his mouth found her center.

"Jasper, oh. Ah, Jasper." She writhed against him as his tongue and fingers stroked her most sensitive place. "I'm going…." She tugged his head away from her pearl. "It's too much."

He gave her his most wicked grin. "Let it happen, love." Then lowered his head back into the cradle of her thighs. He suckled and teased until she came apart, moaning his name as her head pressed into the pillows.

Jasper kissed his way over her stomach, across her ribs, and over the place where her heartbeat rapidly. Then, with one smooth thrust, he buried his cock in her warmth. Stilling, he met her gaze. "You belong to me."

She nodded, her breaths coming rapidly. "Make love to me."

And he did. Jasper made love to her until they were both depleted of energy and full of satisfaction.

Then he pulled her close and stroked his fingers up and down her back. "I will love you forever," he said into the mass of blond curls spread across his chest.

"And I you," she said moments before her eyes closed and soft breaths feathered across his skin.

Jasper smoothed her hair and kissed the top of her head. "Sleep, sweeting," He whispered as the first light of morning filtered into the bedchamber. For the first time in his life, he was truly happy. She was his soulmate. His one and only. The woman God had made just for him. And he was indeed a lucky man.

Epilogue

Christmas,
Five years later,

Celia's breath caught when her gaze found Jasper's. He sat on the sofa with their children gathered around. His cravat was around William's neck, and Mary was sitting on his knee as he read them a Christmas story. The vision left her breathless.

He glanced up and smiled at her after reading the last sentence. "They wanted to hear a story before bed."

"Papa, let us have another cake, too," Mary announced as she hugged Jasper.

Celia grinned. "That does not surprise me." She

shot Jasper a playful look of reproach before turning her attention back to the children. "Alas, it is past your bedtimes."

"One more carol before we go. Please, Mama?" William asked, his green eyes pleading.

Mary slid off of Jasper's knee. "Yes, please?"

"Well, it is Christmas," Celia said, pretending to consider the children's request. "What do you think, Papa?" She asked Jasper, her voice teasing.

"I say we let them sing," he announced, then stood and went to the pianoforte.

Celia settled onto the bench beside him. "Which carol shall I play?"

"Joy to the World," Mary said in a sing-song fashion. "I do so love that one."

William nodded his agreement.

Celia danced her fingers over the ivory keys as Jasper wrapped his arm around her waist. Together with their children, they sang.

"Let every heart prepare him room. And heaven and nature sing, and heaven and nature sing…."

She watched her children with awe and wonder as they sang the words. William, much like his father in both looks and mannerisms, Mary a carbon copy of her. She wondered what the babe growing in her womb would be like.

"Joy to the world, now we sing...."

Her voice trailed off at the thought, and she fought the tears of joy pricking at her eyes.

"Let the angel voices ring."

She beamed at her children as they sang the last words. Happiness filled her to the point of bursting. She never would have guessed her long ago misadventure would have led to a lifetime of love. A doting husband, the sweetest children in the world, and more happiness than one person had a right to. She'd been blessed beyond imagining.

"Off to bed now." Jasper stood and placed his hand on William's shoulder. He nodded at the nanny, and she came forward to usher the children away, but not before Celia and Jasper kissed them goodnight.

Once the children had gone, Celia gave Jasper a flirtatious glance. "I have one more gift for you."

He slid closer. "Does it involve our bedchamber?"

"You're incorrigible." She swatted at him playfully.

"Only for you, sweetheart." He pulled her close and kissed her soundly.

Celia guided his hand to her belly and splayed her fingers over his. "We are expecting another babe."

"That is the best present you could ever give me." He stroked her cheek with the pad of his thumb. "You make my life complete. I love you, Celia. Today, tomorrow, always."

She gave a saucy grin. "Prove it."

He took her in his arms, and she knew he would do that very thing.

Dive into a new series today!
Book 1 in Amanda's Fated For a Rogue series is available now:

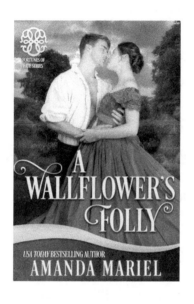

A headstrong woman and a newly minted duke find themselves entangled in a battle of wills and a collision of hearts that defies their predetermined destiny.

A spirited wallflower…

Lady Olivia Montague, a woman unafraid to defy convention, has chosen to embrace spinsterhood rather than be tethered to a dormant engagement.

Her determination to lead life on her own terms is unshakable—until an unexpected reunion upends her solitary existence.

A resolute Duke...

William Breckenridge, now the Duke of Thorne following the tragic loss of his parents, must navigate not only the aristocratic responsibilities thrust upon him but also the care of his three younger sisters. Desperate for help, he recalls his long-neglected betrothal, envisioning a partnership that could ease his familial burdens.

A love unyielding...

As destiny reunites William and Olivia, a battle commences—one that pits their stubborn wills against undeniable desires. With every clash, their mutual attraction deepens, threatening to breach the walls of resistance they've erected. As their hearts become entwined, can they overcome pride and hesitation to seize their destined happily ever after?

Chapter 1

Yorkshire England, 1810

Lady Olivia Montague strolled across the parlor, her slippers threatening to wear through the carpet from her constant pacing. She could scarcely believe what was happening. Why now? Why, after all this time? For Heaven's sake, it had been more than fifteen years since they'd last heard from the duke.

What the devil changed his mind? She turned her attention toward her friends, Lady Emma, and Lady Juliet. "I have to find a way out of this farce, and you ladies are going to help me."

"I fail to see what the problem is," Emma said

from where she sat near the hearth, her violet eyes cool and calm.

Juliet sprang to her feet, pale blond curls bouncing with the movement. "I understand perfectly, but perhaps if you tried to see the situation in a more positive light."

Olivia turned to peer at her well-meaning friends. Lady Emma Finch and Lady Juliet Gale were both the daughters of Earls and longtime family friends. The three of them had been nearly inseparable throughout the years. Honestly, they were more like sisters than friends. And while Olivia knew the pair meant well, she could not help being cross with them at the moment.

She narrowed her eyes as she replied, "You need not understand, and there is nothing positive about this…this…atrocity."

"Now, that is a fine way to describe your pending marriage." Emma shook her head, her lips pressed tightly together.

Juliet sighed, her shoulder's rounding a fraction before she perked back up. "What if you were to fall in love with him? That would be a positive outcome."

Olivia dismissed Juliet's words even as she spoke them. "I will not fall in love with anyone, least of all him." Exasperated, she released a breath, then returned to pacing. "I'm not going to marry him."

The thud of Emma's fan against the arm of the gold brocade wing chair she sat in drew Olivia's attention back to her. "You cannot be serious. There's a betrothal agreement. You're legally bound. You'd face ruination if you refused."

"And besides, he's a duke." Juliet smiled, her blue eyes twinkling. "Every woman dreams of being a duchess."

Olivia could not deny the merits of her friend's arguments, but neither did she believe they applied to her. She tossed her head as she turned back to them. "I don't give a fig what he is, and I don't want to be a duchess."

More than a little frustrated, she dropped onto a nearby settee. "All I want is a way out of this. Hell's teeth, I don't know the first thing about the man. I don't even know what he looks like, and I'm expected to marry him."

Olivia brought her hand to her forehead and began massaging her temples with her thumb and middle finger. Her head pounded, but she did not have time to rest or drink tonics. She had to use every moment to find a way out of her impending marriage.

Juliet leaned forward, a scowl etching lines around her mouth. "Now you are being unfair. He's not a complete stranger. You have met him before. You told us as much."

Olivia dropped her hand to her lap and peered at Juliet. "As I recall, I told you how much I detested him. He was rude, obnoxious, messy, entitled—"

"He was young, a child just like yourself," Emma interrupted, one side of her lips tilting up in the semblance of a smirk. "Truly, Olivia, you should at least give him a chance."

Juliet's expression took on a dreamy quality, all serenity and joy as she looked at Olivia. "What if he's grown into a handsome man with exemplary behavior?" She clasped her hands together with barely contained excitement. "What if he arrives and sweeps you right off your feet?"

Olivia shook her head and squeezed her eyes together. "I assure you, that will not happen."

Emma tipped her head up toward the ceiling, almost as though she were praying, then said, "But it could. If only you'd give him a chance."

Olivia would wager her friend had indeed been lifting a prayer. After all, Emma had always been the most level-headed among them. If her parents asked her to wed a gentleman of their choosing, she'd do so without complaint.

Juliet smiled at Emma before returning her attention to Olivia. "She is right, and you know it. A lot can change with the passage of years. How long has it been? Ten, Twelve years?"

"Fifteen," Olivia forced the word through clenched teeth. Fifteen long years with nary a word from the man. Fifteen years of Olivia believing he'd forgotten her. How the devil did anyone expect her to forget that?

Emma pushed a stray lock of raven-colored hair from her cheek. "The boy you remember has long since grown into a man. I'd wager he has changed a great deal."

"None of this matters. It's all beside the point." Olivia waved her hand in dismissal. "Even if he were handsome and well-mannered, it would not negate the fact that he spent the last fifteen years ignoring our betrothal. Neither my family nor myself received any communication from him or his. I believed myself free."

"Perhaps he had a good reason?" Juliet said, optimism flashing in her blue gaze.

"You both know that I do not wish to marry anyone… ever. And now," Olivia released a deep sigh, "now I am enslaved once more. I cannot bear it. I will not. You have to help me."

Emma clasped Olivia's hands in hers and offered a reassuring smile. "Then we shall, at least as much as we are able."

"Oh, I know. Let's go to the fair." Juliet turned an excited grin on them, bouncing in her seat. "I'm told there's a fortune teller there. You can see her, and maybe she'll tell you what you're supposed to do."

Olivia perked up at the idea and smiled at her friend. "At the very least, she can give me some guidance."

Juliet had always believed in such things, while Emma called them pure nonsense. Olivia did not hold any firm opinions about the unknown. Still, she believed that some people were blessed with unique intuitions and abilities.

She believed it possible that the fortuneteller could tell her something useful, leastwise, she was willing to reserve judgment until she'd seen the woman. What could it hurt?

"Perhaps," Emma released Olivia's hand with a sigh, "though it's far more likely she'll provide nothing more than a moment's entertainment."

Juliet glared at Emma for a heartbeat, then shook her head. "You needn't always be so serious."

"You well know how I feel about such things. I do not want to get Olivia's hopes up." Emma stood. "Shall we be on our way, then?"

Juliet stood, then threaded her arm through Olivia's and leaned closer. "Ignore her, there's nothing wrong with hope."

Olivia gave a slight grin, not wanting to dampen Juliet's excitement, but she well knew that Emma's warning had merit. She looped her arm through Emma's and gave a slight squeeze. "Regardless of how this turns out, I thank you both."

As they made their way from the parlor, Olivia's heart pounded, a mixture of foreboding and excitement turning her insides to knots. Even if the fortune teller had nothing good—nothing helpful to say—Olivia would escape the future being forced on her.

She had to. She'd not settle for any other outcome.

The fairgrounds were all a bustle with the local gentry and common-born folks alike. Olivia's heart fairly pounded free of her chest as she and her friends made their way through the crush in search of the fortuneteller's wagon. They did not have far to go before they spotted it.

Olivia experienced a moment of hesitation as she

stood before the brightly colored wagon with her friends beside her. What if the fortuneteller had nothing good to say? Could Olivia discount her words and move on? Or would they ring through her mind despite her efforts? Perhaps not knowing would be best.

A dark-haired woman with probing brown eyes appeared in the door. "Do not tarry, child," she said as she stepped aside to allow them entrance.

Juliet nudged Olivia, setting her in motion. She took a few tentative steps, then mounted the stairs leading into the conveyance. Juliet and Emma followed close behind her.

"Sit." The fortuneteller indicated a bright velvet bench.

Juliet gave Olivia an encouraging nod while Emma gave a slight grin.

Olivia moved to the bench and lowered herself onto it. Emma and Juliet came to sit beside her, their hips pressed together so they would all fit.

The fortuneteller sat on a bench opposite them. A small table stood between them with a deck of cards sitting nearest the woman. "I am Madame Zeta, and you are?" She smiled, her freckled cheek's rising with the movement.

"Olivia." She cleared her throat and said, "Lady

Olivia Montague." She glanced around the wagon at the brightly colored interior. It was unlike anything she'd seen before, though she found something about it inviting. The tension in her muscles waned as she returned her attention to Madame Zeta.

"I assume you are here to have your fortune told?"

Olivia hesitated for a heartbeat. She nodded, then reached into her reticule and produced three shillings. "Yes, please."

The honey-skinned lady reached across the table, and Olivia dropped the coins into her palm.

Madame Zeta turned, dropping the shillings into a small box at her side. "Very good." She reached out once more. "Give me your hand?"

Though Olivia's pulse quickened, she did not hesitate as she turned her hand over and placed it in Madame Zeta's. Something about the woman put her at ease. Perhaps her warm gaze or the intelligence she saw within it? Maybe the fortuneteller's gentle smiles?

Madame Zeta examined Olivia's palm, then she trailed one dark finger across the lines of Olivia's flesh. A warm tickle resulted, but Olivia held still and remained quiet.

"Your path is well defined but not so much so

that it cannot be altered." Madame Zeta's gaze remained on Olivia's palm as she spoke. "We all have a path to travel. The path of life. It keeps us steady, come what may."

Olivia nibbled on her lower lip as she waited for the woman to say more.

"You are facing a crossroad." Madame Zeta met Olivia's gaze.

Olivia swallowed past the dryness in her throat. "Yes."

"It is a matter of the heart," Madame Zeta said, a knowing flicker in her gaze.

Olivia could only nod as she stared at the intriguing woman.

Madame Zeta wrapped her fingers around Olivia's hand and gave a gentle squeeze. "Love will come to you on the wings of folly. The choice you make will determine your fortune, child. Beware of hasty decisions."

Olivia stared back at her, trying to decipher the meaning of Madame Zeta's words, but they made little sense to her. She released a pent-up breath and asked, "What does that mean? What am I to do?"

Madame Zeta released her hand, and Olivia felt a sudden rush of cold. "That is for you to determine."

"But—"

Madame Zeta shook her head, then stood. "No one else can walk your path, child."

Olivia stared at her with a thousand questions ringing through her mind. Surely there was something more the woman could tell her. Some sort of guidance she could give. "Please?" Olivia asked with more desperation than she'd intended.

"I can foretell no more child."

Emma stood and reached for Olivia's arm, giving a slight tug. "Let us be on our way."

"Indeed." Juliet sprang to her feet with a broad smile.

Olivia rose to join them, then departed the wagon with a heavy heart. Madame Zeta's words had been a riddle, and she didn't know how she was to solve it, but somehow she must.

Chapter 2

෨෬

William Breckenridge, Duke of Thorne, lounged near a large floor to ceiling window in the Marquess of Pemberton's library as he awaited an audience with the lord. With his gaze trained on the door, he straightened his cravat.

What the devil was keeping Lord Pemberton? His butler had shown William to the library upon his arrival. Now more than twenty minutes had passed, and William detested waiting.

William stood and turned to gaze out the window as he wondered how long Pemberton would keep him in suspense. He rubbed a hand over his jaw, contemplating.

After William's fifteen-year absence, he didn't

suppose he had any grounds for complaint, regardless of how long it took the marquess to appear. Patience is a virtue, he reminded himself. Cliché, but also true.

Releasing a breath, William turned his thoughts toward his purpose for being here. He could not help but marvel at the fact he'd finally come for his bride. He'd always known he'd marry. As a duke, it was his duty to do so. But he'd not been in any hurry to see it done. Rather, he resented the fact that his life had been arranged.

But now everything had changed. William needed to claim his wife with all due haste and could only hope Pemberton felt the same way. That the man would turn his daughter over, honor their agreement without issue. Could William blame him if he refused?

And what of the lady?

Surely Lady Olivia would pose no objection, for what woman did not dream of her wedding day? She'd probably spent most of her life wishing he'd arrive and waiting to call herself duchess. After all, the two of them had been betrothed as children. Their lives all planned out and handed to them on silver platters.

William had long detested the fact that when the

time came, he would have to take the mousey chit to wife, and done all he could to resist and delay. How odd that he now found himself grateful for the arraignment.

With his parents passed on and three sisters to care for, he desperately needed a woman's guidance. Not for himself, but for his hellion sisters. Two of whom were of an age to have their come outs. A neatly packaged wife would suit his needs. Save him from all that awaited.

A shiver of repulsion went through him. He could not imagine having to escort his sisters around to countless balls, soirees, musicals, and such. He scarcely believed himself capable of guarding and guiding them.

Hell would be far preferable.

Though his worries did not begin and end with the social aspects of his sisters stepping into society. No, they were more profound than that. His sisters required a mother figure to guide them and see that they had the things young ladies needed. Someone to keep them on the right path. A lady they could look up to. One they could take their troubles to.

A portrait of a young girl caught William's attention, and he strolled across the library to gain a better vantage point. There on the wall, in a large gilded frame, hung a painting of Lady Olivia. She looked to be around ten years old and just as he remembered. Gangly, her hair in braids and her body long and flat.

He desperately hoped she'd grown some curves.

Regardless, Lady Olivia would serve his purpose as well as any lady could.

More importantly, there was no need to waste time courting—he wasn't required to woo her—this would be a quick and straightforward affair. He would do his duty, then take his wife home to see after his sisters and manage his house. In exchange, Lady Olivia would gain the title of duchess, a generous allowance, and the run of his estates. Once he secured his heir, she'd have all the freedom he could afford her.

"Your Grace." Lord Pemberton entered the room and bowed.

William returned the greeting, encouraged by the good cheer reflected on Pemberton's face. It seemed his soon to be father-in-law wasn't holding a grudge.

William grinned at the older man before saying, "I imagine you know why I have come?"

"Indeed. Your letter arrived safely, and we are very much looking forward to the joining of our families." Pemberton moved to his desk and nodded at a velvet chair across from it. "Please make yourself comfortable."

William took the seat, then accepted a tumbler of brandy. "Will Lady Olivia be joining us?"

"Ah, yes. My wife has gone to fetch her." Pemberton shuffled some papers on his desk. "In the meantime, did you wish to review the marriage contract?"

"There's no need." William had read the blasted thing thousands of times since its creation. Before his parents' deaths, they had often reminded him of his duty and hounded him to see to his marriage. A stab of regret pierced him. He should have honored their wishes while they still lived. He added, "I'm well acquainted with its contents and see no reason to alter the terms."

"I have objections." A feminine voice rang out from somewhere behind him, and William turned to see a dark-haired beauty standing beside an older but equally attractive woman. He rose to greet them.

"Olivia," Pemberton warned as he came to his feet.

William raised a hand to silence the man. "It's quite all right."

"Nonsense." Lady Pemberton strolled further

into the library, coming to stand beside her husband. "Please excuse our daughter's ill-manor. I assure you we have raised her to behave as a proper lady ought to, Your Grace."

"I've already forgiven the misstep." William bowed to Lady Olivia. "My lady."

"Your Grace." She peered back at him through fiery amber eyes before dipping a curtsey.

William stared at her, half-amused, and part vexed. What had happened to the wallflower he remembered? The awkward girl with arms and limbs too long for her thin frame?

The woman peering at him scarcely resembled the girl he'd been promised. Her temper most certainly did not. He attempted to cajole her with a rakish grin, but she only scowled more fiercely. Her displeasure plain for all to witness.

William took a step toward her. "Please voice your objection."

The Marchioness paled, her eyes rounding as she turned her head to stare at her daughter. "She has none." Lady Pemberton wrapped her arm around Lady Olivia's shoulders. "Isn't that right?"

Despite the question, William could tell by the way Lady Pemberton glared at Lady Olivia that it wasn't really a question that required an answer. To her credit, Lady Olivia met his gaze and said, "Actually, I do."

The Marchioness turned porcelain, not a stitch of color remaining in her face, but Lady Olivia paid her no mind as she continued laying voice to her objection. "I have no wish to marry a stranger."

Her father came around his desk, his cheeks flushed. "The duke is no stranger. You have been acquainted from childhood and betrothed just as long."

"I beg to differ. I've not received so much as a letter in the past fifteen years. I do not know the duke at all." Lady Olivia pressed her lips together and glared at William. "And I have no wish to marry him."

William eased closer to Lady Olivia and said, "She's right."

Lord and Lady Pemberton turned to him, their mouths agape. Lord Pemberton recovered first. He placed a hand on his wife's arm, but his gaze remained riveted on William as he said, "Surely you do not mean—"

"And we shall have a lifetime to correct my oversight," William added, cutting the marquess off. He returned his attention to Lady Olivia, offering what he hoped was a reassuring smile. "I intend to honor my parent's wishes. I've secured a special license so we can marry with haste. Afterward, we can spend as much time as you please getting reacquainted."

Her eyes rounded, the copper flecks darkening. "You wish to marry at once?"

"Indeed," William answered.

Lady Olivia back stepped and turned panicked eyes on her father. "Surely waiting for the bans to be read is not asking too much."

"Dearest," her father crossed over to her and took her hands. "You are betrothed and will ultimately be wed, what difference does it make if the ceremony takes place tonight or three weeks from now?"

"It makes a world of difference." She turned her beseeching gaze on William. "Please. Allow us to wait for the banns?"

"If that is your wish, I shall honor it."

William surprised himself with the words more than anyone else. He could not say why he'd agreed, only that something in the way she pleaded tugged at his heart.

He had no wish to make her unhappy. That had never been his goal. In fact, he hoped that in time they would develop a care for one another. Regardless, he intended to be a good husband. He may not have chosen her, but he'd not make her suffer because of it.

If waiting for the banns to be read set her at ease, then that is what they would do. In the meantime, William would strive to win her over.

About the Author

Amanda Mariel, an accomplished wordsmith, holds dual master's degrees in liberal arts and education, specializing in the captivating realms of history and literature. Beyond her academic pursuits, she embraces the joyful chaos of motherhood, tending to both her cherished teenagers and her trio of adored fur babies. Among them, a noble Bernese Mountain Dog named Blaze, and two cats of distinct character, Ezra and Puff, share their home.

A USA Today Bestselling luminary, Amanda Mariel conjures vivid tapestries of eras long past, drawing inspiration from the languid cadence of days gone by. With pen poised and imagination unfurled, she traverses the annals of time, weaving tales that illuminate historical landscapes with finesse and flair. Her creative spirit finds respite in reading, traversing new horizons through travel, and capturing moments through the lenses of both her camera and artistic endeavors. Yet, it is in the embrace of family that she finds her truest sanctuary.

To delve deeper into Amanda's captivating world visit www.amandamariel.com. While there, an invitation to join her newsletter promises a gateway to the latest from Amanda Mariel's literary treasury, and an opportunity to claim a complimentary eBook.

Amanda's passion extends to her readers, welcoming their voices and stories into her narrative realm. Engage with her through email at amanda@amandamariel.com, or connect via her social Media channels.

Facebook: facebook.com/AuthorAmandaMarie1
Twitter: twitter.com/AmandaMarieAuth
BookBub: bookbub.com/authors/amanda-mariel
Instagram: instagram.com/authoramandamariel
TicTok: tiktoc.com/@amandamarielromance

Amidst the prose and parchment, Amanda Mariel etches a profound connection, bridging eras, hearts, and minds, creating a legacy that resonates through the corridors of time.

Also by Amanda Mariel

Ladies and Scoundrels series

Scandalous Endeavors

Scandalous Intentions

Scandalous Redemption

Scandalous Wallflower

Scandalous Liaison

Dancing with Serendipity

Fabled Love Series

Enchanted by the Earl

Captivated by the Captain

Enticed by Lady Elianna

Delighted by the Duke

Lady Archer's Creed series

Amanda Mariel writing with Christina McKnight

Theodora

Georgina

Adeline

Josephine

Scandal Meets Love series

Love Only Me

Find Me Love

If it's Love

Odd's of Love

Believe in Love

Chance of Love

Love and Holly

Love and Mistletoe

A Rogue's Kiss Series

Her Perfect Rogue

His Perfect Hellion

This Rogue of Mine

Her Perfect Scoundrel

Wicked Earls' Club

Titles by Amanda Mariel

Earl of Grayson

Earl of Edgemore

Earl of Persuasion

Earl of Stone (Fated for a Rogue)

These are designed so they can standalone

How to Kiss a Rogue (Amanda Mariel)

A Kiss at Christmastide (Christina McKnight)

A Wallflower's Christmas Kiss (Dawn Brower)

Stealing a Rogue's Kiss (Amanda Mariel)

Scandalized by a Rogue's Kiss (Amanda Mariel)

A Gypsy's Christmas kiss (Dawn Brower)

A Vixen's Christmas kiss (Dawn Brower)

Standalone titles

One Moonlit Tryst

One Enchanting Kiss

Christmas in the Duke's Embrace

One Wicked Christmas

A Lyon in Her Bed (The Lyon's Den connected world)

Courting Temptation (House of Devon connected world)

Forever My Rogue (Love Be a Lady's Charm Connected World)

Box sets and anthologies

Visit www.amandamariel.com to see Amanda's current offerings.

Thank you so much for taking the time to read *Her Perfect Scoundrel.*

Your opinion matters!

Please take a moment to review this book on your favorite review site and share your opinion with fellow readers.

USA Today bestselling author Amanda Mariel

~Heartwarming historical romances that leave you breathless~